LAURA SECORD'S
BRAVE WALK

by
Connie Brummel Crook

june lawrason

illustrated by
June Lawrason

SECOND
STORY
Press

"Laura," James Secord said, "I must help fight to save our country. General Brock needs more soldiers; I will be one of them."

Laura was very sad when her husband said this, but she replied, "Be careful. Here, take my locket to remember me even when you are in battle."

It was June 1812, and a great fear had fallen over Upper and Lower Canada. The United States to the south had just declared war on the young British colony. People everywhere were preparing for battle and protecting their homes and forts.

At the western edge of the Niagara Peninsula, near Niagara Falls, there was a town called Queenston. Laura Secord lived there with her husband, James, and their children in a new white wooden house on the east bank of the Niagara River. Behind it was Queenston Heights, a steep hill covered with many trees: oak, maple, willow, pine and spruce.

One morning just before daybreak, Laura woke up suddenly. Rain pelted against the window in the pitch darkness of the October night. She was almost certain she had heard firing. Her heart beat faster as she thought of the danger so close — even on Queenston Heights.

"Mama, Mama," little Charles cried out in fright from his box-bed in the hall. Laura grabbed Baby Appy from her cradle and rushed to Charles and her older daughters, Mary, Charlotte and Harriet.

"Hurry," she said as she led them down to the dug-out cold cellar below their house.

She lit a small candle and set it on a high shelf. "You'll be safe here," she said, trying to comfort her frightened children.

Then she climbed back up the steep ladder to the hallway above. Cannons and muskets roared deafeningly all around. Laura sat in the darkness and prayed for James.

Then silence surrounded the house. Laura crept to the back door, pulled the bolt, and looked outside. The smell of sulphur from the guns hung thick in the damp air.

A bolt of lightning streaked across the sky, lighting up a soldier from James's militia. He limped towards the house.

"Thank you," he gasped as Laura helped him through the doorway. "The fighting has stopped ... until we get more supplies. But our general ... General Brock has been killed ... and James is wounded ... He's behind enemy lines — just behind the cannon."

"James — wounded!" Laura began to tremble. She rushed headlong out the door and climbed the hill to the battlefield. Frantically she ran among the enemy soldiers, searching everywhere for James. Suddenly she saw a soldier raise his musket at a fallen man — James!

"No!" she screamed in terror, and threw herself down over her husband.

"Stop!" The sharp command rang out from a short distance up the hill. As the enemy soldier stared into the face of his own leader, he lowered his musket.

Laura looked fearfully up at the American officer.

"Let the woman take her husband home," he barked.

Laura knelt beside James. He had bullet wounds in his knee and shoulder, and could not move. Eventually the officer and a soldier carried James back to their house, Laura walking anxiously beside them.

Months passed, and James's wounds did not heal. Laura did her best to nurse him back to health, but the war worried them both. The British were losing. In the spring the Americans captured York, then swept around the western tip of the Niagara Peninsula over Burlington Bay and on to Newark. They took Fort George just north of Queenston and were also advancing from the south. Almost all the Niagara Peninsula had been captured — except for a small place, called Beaver Dams.

One hot June night after the children were in bed, Laura was helping James walk upstairs. They had been talking about Beaver Dams and its defender, Lieutenant James FitzGibbon.

"Why do the Americans call him the Green Sliver?" Laura asked.

James paused to catch his breath. "Green because he's Irish, though he trained under the British General Brock, and Sliver because they want to make light of his threat to them."

Loud knocking at the front door interrupted them.

"Enemy soldiers looking for food again, no doubt," Laura muttered. The knocking became louder. The soldiers were shouting and jeering. "Dear God, protect us," she prayed as she rushed back down the stairs.

With trembling hands, Laura opened the door and looked up into the cold blue eyes of a tall man. "Evening, ma'am," he said roughly. "I've got some hungry men here. Tonight it's your turn to fix them supper."

Queenston was now surrounded by Americans. No one could disobey an American officer. "Supper will be ready in half an hour," said Laura, leading them into her parlour.

While she worked, her mind raced. She had recognized the blue-eyed man: he was Cyrenius Chapin, the famous American military leader. If *he* was in town, something important must be happening. "I *must* find out their plans!" she thought.

By the time the meal was ready, Laura had an idea. The men slid eagerly along the benches on each side of the kitchen table and began reaching for the food. They took big gulps from their cups and broke into grins.

"Hard apple cider! Why, that's mighty generous of you, ma'am," said Chapin and held out his cup for more.

Laura poured, then set the jug on the table. "I've got chores to do," she said loudly. "When you're done, you can let yourselves out."

Laura scuffled along the gravel path that led to the bake-oven shed at the back of the house. Then she stepped onto the grass and crept back to the kitchen window. Just as she had hoped, the hard cider and good food had relaxed the men and made them talkative.

"That Green Sliver is getting too bold, sir," a voice said.

"Do you think Colonel Boerstler will take your advice?"

"Of course he will. He'd be a fool not to," Chapin bragged. "Now's our chance to get rid of that Green Sliver and his soldiers."

"So, Captain, we attack the day after tomorrow?"

"Yes. We'll combine forces with Boerstler's troops at Fort George and march down on Beaver Dams. When that's wiped out, Upper Canada will be ours!"

Laura stole away from the window. The men must not know that she had heard their secret plans. She waited by the well at the side of the house until she heard the front door slam and saw them leave.

Then she hurried back into the house and up the stairs.

"James," Laura whispered as she shook her husband's shoulder. "Listen to me!"

James turned over in his bed and groaned in pain. The wound in his knee still hurt badly.

"James," Laura went on, "those soldiers are planning to attack FitzGibbon at Beaver Dams!"

Instantly, he was wide awake.

"I overheard it! James, somebody ought to tell Lieutenant FitzGibbon!"

James fell back on his pillow. "I would go, Laura, if only I could," he groaned. "But even if I crawled on my hands and knees, I could not get there in time."

"I could," Laura said.

James stared up at her fearfully.

"Don't worry," Laura said. "God will take care of me."

After only a few hours' sleep, Laura got up and dressed, then went to look at each of her sleeping children. When she came to her husband, he was already awake. She grasped his hand and held it tightly.

Their eyes met. "God go with you, Laura," he whispered.

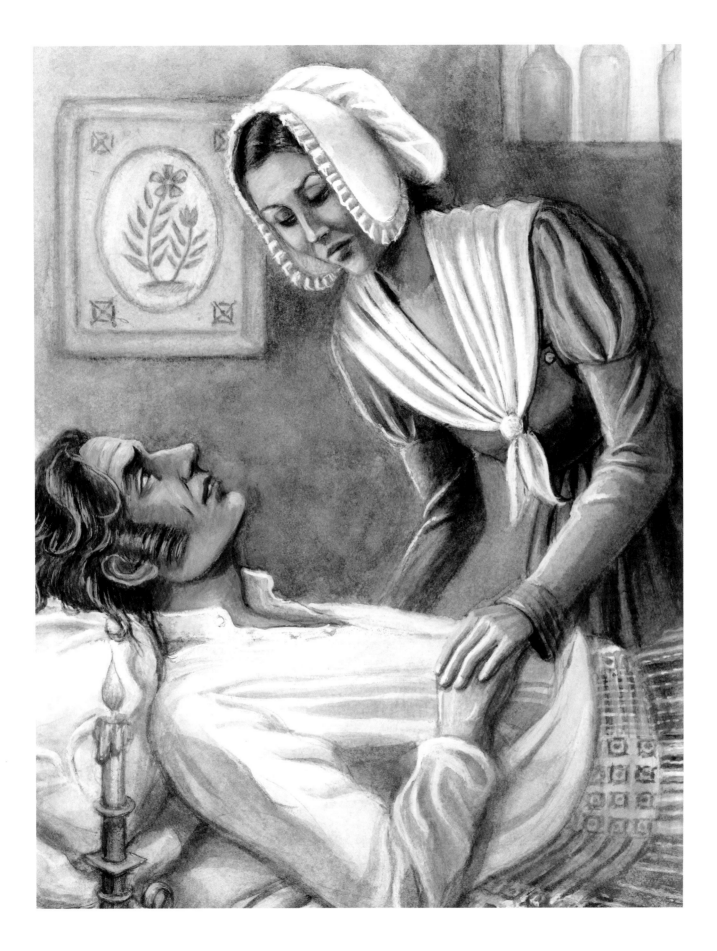

The sun was barely up as Laura slipped out the back door into the dawn. She hurried along a cow trail, heading west towards St. David's and the Great Black Swamp. It was not the shortest way, but it was the only route to take. The enemy soldiers would not let her pass along the main road.

She jumped down from the rail fence onto the path. "Halt!" an American guard shouted. "Where do you think you're going?"

Laura had a good story ready. "I'm going to visit my brother, Charles Ingersoll. He is wounded and sick at the home of Hannah Secord, a widow in St. David's."

The guard knew this was true, but he hesitated. Laura held her breath.

"Why are you leaving so early? The sun is just rising."

"It's cooler now. I would faint if I travelled later, in the heat of the day."

The guard stepped closer to look at Laura. She was pale and thin. He nodded and let her go on.

Two hours later, Laura had found a sturdy branch for a walking stick and pushed her way into the swamp. Branches caught and tore at her skirt. Mosquitoes and horseflies swarmed around her. But she plodded on, always testing the oozing, wet ground ahead with her stick.

When the ground finally became firmer, Laura leaned against a large rock to rest.

"Ch-ch-ch-ch-ch!"

She froze. A rattler!

Then she heard a rustle and caught a glimpse of the snake before it slithered away. Laura began to run.

A quarter-mile later, her right foot suddenly sank beneath her in quicksand!

Balancing herself with her stick and with one foot on solid ground, she managed to wrench her foot free. But her shoe was lost! She stood and watched in despair as it disappeared slowly into the mud.

At last, Laura struggled up out of the swamp and into the light and strong heat of the day. Turning onto the road that led to Beaver Dams, she smiled weakly with relief. Although she still had to cross Twelve Mile Creek, the thought of its cool, clear waters was refreshing.

It was dusk when Laura reached the creek; it was running fast like a river, nearly overflowing its banks. She was lucky — a tree had fallen across it like a bridge. Laura struggled onto the trunk.

As she crawled along it, her cap caught on an overhanging branch; her thick brown hair hung down in wet strings. Just as she was halfway across, a rush of water washed her other shoe away and wrapped the hem of her petticoat around the stub of a branch. She tore it loose and inched forward.

Finally, she dared to put a foot down into the water and waded towards the shore. She parted the last bunch of reeds and scrambled up onto the grassy bank.

Laura pushed wearily up the hill through the grass and weeds. She winced as she stepped on a sharp stone she didn't see, but the throbbing of her foot was lost in the pain she felt all over her body.

At the top of the hill, she stifled a sharp cry. At least a dozen men were coming towards her, some wearing Mohawk leggings. She shook as she faced the Chief squarely.

"Please take me to Lieutenant FitzGibbon," she said, knowing his camp should be just over the hill.

The Chief gestured; she was to follow him. Two of his men paced swiftly beside her, and soon Laura's breath was coming in short gasps. Then, in the moonlight, she saw the top of a chimney poking up over the hill.

FitzGibbon himself emerged from the front door of his headquarters.

Laura staggered forward and choked out, "I am the wife of Sergeant James Secord, who was wounded at the Battle of Queenston Heights. Unable to travel, he sends this message. The enemy under Colonel Boerstler, and directed by Chapin's fighters, plan a surprise attack tomorrow. They have a much larger force than you."

The lieutenant's cool green eyes narrowed. "How could you possibly have come by the road? Enemy scouts are patrolling all the way to Queenston along that route."

"I came through the Great Black Swamp. Then I went south across Twelve Mile Creek to the Mohawks' camp."

FitzGibbon looked down at Laura's bare, scratched feet. He saw her skirt, hanging in wet and muddy tatters around her ankles, and he studied her sunburned, mosquito-bitten face. She gazed steadfastly back at him. He could not doubt her sincerity, she thought. She had risked her life to bring him this secret message.

"That's nineteen miles in this burning heat!" FitzGibbon said at last. Then he handed his lantern to a soldier. "Take this woman to rest at that farmhouse next door," he commanded.

Laura let out her breath. He believed her! He believed she had come those nineteen miles! Now FitzGibbon and his men would have a chance to save Upper Canada.

Her steps steadied, and she raised her head proudly as she walked away.

She had delivered her message. She had done it!

To Cynthia Rankin, whose courage, vision and compassion match those of Laura Secord
— C.B.C.

To Doug, Derek and Alex
— J.L.

CANADIAN CATALOGUING IN PUBLICATION DATA
Crook, Connie Brummel
Laura Secord's brave walk

ISBN 1-896764-34-7 (bound)

1. Secord, Laura, 1775-1868 — Juvenile fiction. I Lawrason, June. II. Title

PS8555.R6113L37 2000   jC813'.54   C00-931102-5
PZ7.C8818La 2000

Edited by Sean Oakey
Printed in Hong Kong

Second Story Press gratefully acknowledges the assistance of the Ontario Arts
Council and The Canada Council for the Arts for our publishing program.
We acknowledge the financial support of the Government of Canada through the
Book Publishing Industry Development Program (BPIDP) for our publishing activities.

SECOND STORY PRESS
720 Bathurst Street Suite 301
Toronto, Canada M5S 2R4

AUTHOR'S HISTORICAL NOTE

A certificate found in 1959 in the National Archives in Ottawa attests that Laura made her famous journey and informed FitzGibbon of the coming attack. In the certificate, Lieutenant FitzGibbon himself gave the exact date of Laura Secord's walk and drew attention to the fact that her message reached him first. "In consequence of this information," he wrote, "I placed Indians under Norton [the Mohawks' adopted Scottish leader] together with my Detachment in a Situation to intercept the American Detachment."

Laura Secord did not receive recognition for her heroism until she was in her eighties. In 1860, nineteen-year-old Albert Edward, Prince of Wales, visited Niagara Falls and became interested in her story. In 1861, he sent her £100 in gold in appreciation for her service to her country. Prince Albert Edward later became King Edward VII.

NOTES FOR PAGE 14:

"James, ... somebody ought to tell Lieutenant FitzGibbon." Laura Secord as related by Laura Secord Clark, granddaughter of Laura Secord, to Mrs. George S. Henry. Ontario Dept. of Public Records and Archives, Misc., 1933, in Ruth McKenzie, *Laura Secord: The Legend and the Lady* (Toronto: McClelland and Stewart, 1971), p. 51.

" ... if I crawled on my hands and knees, I could not get there in time." James Secord in *Laura Secord*, p. 51.

" ... God will take care of me." Laura Secord in *Laura Secord*, p. 51.

For a dramatized account of Laura Secord's life, read the novel *Laura's Choice* by Connie Brummel Crook (Winnipeg: Windflower Communications, 1993). Order through the National Book Service at 1-800-263-8738 or the publisher at 1-800-465-6564.